The Toy in the Wood

and other toy stories

Compiled by Tig Thomas

Miles
KeLLY

First published in 2014 by Miles Kelly Publishing Ltd
Harding's Barn, Bardfield End Green, Thaxted, Essex, CM6 3PX, UK

Copyright © Miles Kelly Publishing Ltd 2014

2 4 6 8 10 9 7 5 3 1

Publishing Director Belinda Gallagher
Creative Director Jo Cowan
Editorial Director Rosie Neave
Senior Editor Sarah Parkin
Senior Designer Joe Jones
Production Manager Elizabeth Collins
Reprographics Stephan Davis, Jennifer Hunt, Thom Allaway

All rights reserved. No part of this publication may be reproduced, stored in a retrieval system, or transmitted by any means, electronic, mechanical, photocopying, recording or otherwise, without the prior permission of the copyright holder.

ISBN 978-1-78209-461-6

Printed in China

British Library Cataloguing-in-Publication Data
A catalogue record for this book is available from the British Library

ACKNOWLEDGEMENTS

The publishers would like to thank the following artists who have contributed to this book:

Advocate Art: Milena Jahier, Claire Keay (inc. cover), Bruno Merz
Beehive Illustration: Rupert Van Wyk (inc. decorative frames)

Made with paper from a sustainable forest

www.mileskelly.net   info@mileskelly.net

Contents

The Visit to Santa Claus Land

By Anon

JACK AND MARGARET were growing more excited each day, because Christmas was so near. They talked of nothing but Santa Claus.

"Don't you wish you could see him?" they said, over and over.

One night, just before Christmas, Mother

tucked them in bed and left them to go to sleep. But Jack wiggled, Margaret wriggled. At last they both sat up in bed.

"Jack," Margaret whispered, "are you asleep yet?"

"No," said Jack, "I can't go to sleep. Margaret, don't you wish you could see Santa Claus? What's that?"

They both listened, and they heard a little tap, tap on the window. They looked, and there, right in the window, they saw a funny little elf.

"What's that I heard you say? You want to see Santa Claus? Well, I am one of his elves. I am on my way back to Santa Claus Land. I'll take you with me if you really want to go."

Jack and Margaret quickly scrambled from their beds.

"Come on, show us the way!" they cried in great excitement.

"No, indeed," said the elf. "No one must know the way to Santa Claus Land. Kindly wait a moment."

The elf took something soft and thick and dark, and tied it around Jack's eyes. Next he took something soft and thick and dark, and tied it around Margaret's eyes.

"How many fingers before you?" the little elf asked.

Both of them shook their heads. They could not see a wink.

"Very well, now we're off," said the elf.

He took Jack's hand on one side, and

Margaret's on the other. It seemed as if they flew through the window. They went on swiftly for a little while, then the elf whirled them round and round, and off they went again. The children could not tell whether they were going north, south, east or west. After a time they stopped.

"Here we are," said the elf.

He uncovered their eyes and the children saw that they were standing before a big, thick gate.

The elf knocked and the gate swung open. They went through it, right into Santa Claus' garden. There were rows and rows of Christmas trees, all glittering with balls and tinsel, and instead of flower beds there were beds of every kind of toy in the world.

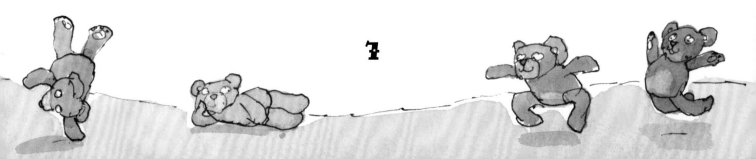

Margaret at once ran over to a bed of dolls.

"Let's see if any of them are ripe," said the elf.

"Ripe?" said Margaret in great surprise.

"Why, of course," said the elf. "Now if this one is ripe it will shut its eyes."

The elf picked a little doll from the bed and laid it in Margaret's arms. Its eyes went half shut and then stuck.

"No, it's not ripe yet," said the elf. "Try this one."

He picked another one, and this one shut its eyes just as if it had gone to sleep.

"We'll take that one," he said, and he dropped it into a big sack he was carrying.

"Come over here, Margaret!" Jack called.

Margaret ran over to another bed and

there were drums – big drums, little drums and middle-sized drums, yellow drums, blue drums, green drums and red drums.

"Can we gather some of these?" said Jack to the elf.

"Of course. Let's see if this one is ripe."

The elf took up a little red drum and gave it a thump with a drum stick. But it made such a strange sound that Jack and Margaret both laughed out loud. The little red drum was put back into the bed and the elf tried another big one. It went Boom! Boom! Boom! Boom! Boom! Jack and Margaret marched along the bed, keeping step to it.

When they had finished picking drums, they went over to a bed filled with horns.

That was the most fun of all. Some of them made very odd noises, and on some the elf played jolly little tunes.

The next bed they came to was filled with toys that could be wound up. There were trains, automobiles, dancing dolls, climbing monkeys, hopping birds, funny wobbling ducks and every kind of toy you could think of. The children stayed at this bed for a long time.

At last Margaret said, "But where is Santa Claus? We wanted to see him."

"Oh, to be sure," said the elf. "Come along," and he led them down a long, winding walk, to the edge of the garden. Then he pointed to a hill in the distance.

"Do you see that large white house?

That is where he lives."

The children stared at it. It was so white that it seemed to shine in the distance.

"Walk right across here," said the elf, "then up the hill to Santa Claus' house."

"Oh, must we walk across there?" said Margaret. She stared down at the deep dark chasm between the garden and the hill. A narrow plank was stretched across it.

"Walk carefully," said the elf, "and mind you don't look down. For if you do, I'm afraid you won't see Santa Claus tonight."

"We'll be very careful," said Jack. "Come along Margaret." He took his little sister's hand and they started across the plank.

They had almost reached the middle of it when Jack looked down.

"Oh!" he said, and gave Margaret a pull. She looked down too, and cried "Oh, Oh!" and down, down, down they went.

Suddenly they landed with a thump. They sat up and rubbed their eyes – they were right in their own beds at home. Mother opened the door.

"Are you awake, children?" she said.

"Oh, Mother, we haven't been asleep. We've been to Santa Claus Land, and we nearly saw Santa Claus!"

Then they told her all about it, and Mother just smiled.

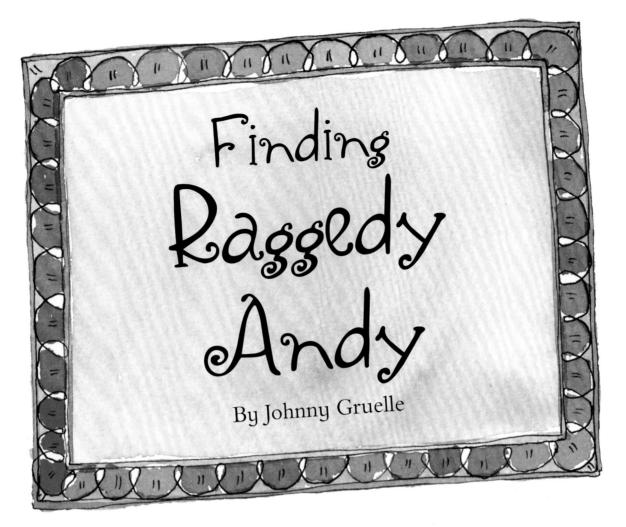

Finding Raggedy Andy

By Johnny Gruelle

The father of Marcella, who is the owner of Raggedy Ann, is an artist, and sometimes he borrows Raggedy Ann to draw pictures of her for children's books.

ONE DAY, DADDY TOOK Raggedy Ann down to his office and propped her up against some books upon his desk. He wanted to have her where he could see her cheery smile all day.

14

Daddy wished to catch a whole lot of Raggedy Ann's cheeriness and happiness, and put all this down on paper. Then those who did not have Raggedy Ann dolls might see just how happy a rag doll can be.

So Raggedy Ann stayed at Daddy's studio for three or four days. She was missed very much at home and Marcella longed for her. But she knew that Daddy was borrowing some of Raggedy Ann's sunshine, so she did not complain.

Raggedy Ann did not complain either, for in addition to the sunny, happy smile she always wore (it was painted on) Raggedy Ann had a candy heart, and no one (not even a rag doll) ever complains if they have such happiness about them.

One evening, just as Daddy was finishing his day's work, a messenger boy came with a package – a nice, soft, lumpy package. Daddy opened it and found a letter.

Grandma had told Daddy, long before this, that at the time Raggedy Ann was made, a neighbour had made a boy doll, Raggedy Andy. She had made him for her little girl, who played with Grandma.

And Grandma told Daddy she had wondered whatever had become of her little playmate and the boy doll, Raggedy Andy.

After reading the letter, Daddy opened the other package, which was inside the nice, soft, lumpy package and found – Raggedy Andy. He had been carefully folded up.

His soft, floppy arms were folded up in front of him, and his soft, floppy legs were folded over his arms. They were held this way by a rubber band.

Raggedy Andy must have wondered why he was being done up this way, but it could not have worried him, for inbetween where his feet came over his face, Daddy saw his cheery smile.

After slipping off the rubber band, Daddy smoothed out the wrinkles in Raggedy Andy's arms and legs. Then he propped Raggedy Ann and Raggedy Andy up against books on his desk, so that they sat facing each other – Raggedy Ann's shoe button eyes looking straight into the shoe button eyes of Raggedy Andy.

They could not speak – not right out before a real person – so they just sat there and smiled at each other.

"So, Raggedy Ann and Raggedy Andy," said Daddy, "I will go away and let you have your visit to yourselves, although it is good to sit and share your happiness by watching you."

Daddy then took the rubber band and placed it around Raggedy Ann's right hand, and around Raggedy Andy's right hand, so that when he had it fixed properly they sat and held each other's hands.

Daddy knew they would wish to tell

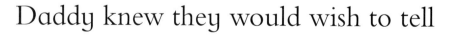

each other all the wonderful things that had happened to them since they had parted more than fifty years before.

So, locking his studio door, Daddy left the two rag dolls looking into each other's eyes.

The next morning, when Daddy unlocked his door and looked at his desk, he saw that Raggedy Andy had fallen over so that he lay with his head in the bend of Raggedy Ann's arm.

The Toys in the Wood

An extract from *The Land of Lost Toys*
by Juliana Horatia Ewing

*A woman, out on a walk, has sat down beneath
a tree she used to play under as a child.*

THE TREE UNDER which I sat was an old friend. There was a hole at its base that I knew well. We always used to say that fairies lived within, but I never saw anything go in apart from wood beetles.

There was one going in at that moment.

I had not noticed until then how much larger the hole was than it used to be.

"I suppose the rain and so forth wears it away over time," I said vaguely.

"I suppose it does," said the beetle politely, "will you walk in?"

I don't know why I was not as astonished as you would imagine. I went.

As I stood inside I caught sight of a large spider crouched up in a corner and said, "Can you tell me, sir, if this is Fairyland?"

"Well," he said, "it's a Province. The fact is, it's the Land of Lost Toys. You haven't such a thing as a fly anywhere about you, have you?"

"No," I said, "I'm sorry to say I don't."

I hurried forward, and reached an open space with lights and music. Toys lay in their places looking so incredibly attractive, when all in a moment, a dozen toy fiddles began to play. It was weird fairy music.

When the music began, all the toys rose. The dolls jumped down and began to dance, the puzzles put themselves together, the bricks built houses, the balls flew from side to side, the skipping ropes went round, whilst a go-cart ran

madly about with nobody inside. The beetle
was once more at my elbow.

"There are beautiful toys here," I said.

"Well, yes," he replied, "and some odd-
looking ones too. You see, whatever
has been well used by a child as a
playing gets a right to come
down here in the end.
Look over there."

I looked, and
said, "It seems to
be a potato."

"So it is," said
the beetle. "It
belonged to an
Irish child in one
of your great cities.

It was the only plaything he ever had. He played with it every day, until he lost it. No toys come down here until they are broken or lost. Look at that box."

"It's my old Toy Box!" I exclaimed.

"You don't mean to say you have any toys here? If you have, the sooner you make your way home the better."

"Why?"

"Well," he said, "there's a very strong feeling in the place. The toys think that they are ill-treated, and not taken care of by children in general. And there is some truth in it. If any of their old masters or mistresses come this way, they shall be punished."

"How will they be punished?" I asked.

"What they did to their toys, their toys

will do to them."

I turned to go, but somehow I lost the road, so I turned back. As I did so, I heard a click – the lid of a small box burst open and up jumped a figure. He was very like my old Jack-in-a-box. My back began to creep, and I tried to remember whether it were my brother or I who came up with the idea of making a small bonfire, and burning the old Jack-in-a-box. At this moment he nodded to me and spoke.

"Oh! It's you, is it?" he said.

"No, it's not," I answered hastily.

"Who is it, then?" he inquired.

"I'm sure I don't know," I said, and really I was so confused that I hardly did.

"Well, we know," said the Jack-in-a-box,

"and that's all that's needed. Now, my friends," he continued, to the toys who had begun to crowd round us, "the hour of our revenge has come."

What was that familiar figure among the rest, in a yellow silk dress? It was my dear doll Rosa. No one could say I had ill-treated her. She fixed her eyes on me with a smile.

"Take notice," shouted the Jack-in-a-box, "that the rule of this court is tit for tat."

"Tie a string round her neck and take her out bathing in the brooks," I heard a voice say. It was my old Dowager Doll.

"It's not fair," I said,

"the string was only to keep you from being carried away by the stream."

"Tear her hair off," shrieked the Dowager. "Flatten her nose!"

A dozen voices shouted for a dozen different punishments, and terrible suggestions were made, which I have forgotten now. I have a vague idea that several voices cried that I was to be sent to be washed in somebody's pocket, and that through all the din the thick voice of my old leather ball repeated,

"Throw her into the dustbin."

Suddenly Rosa spoke up. "My dears," she began, "Let us follow our usual rule. I claim the first turn because I was the prisoner's oldest toy."

"She is right," said the Jack-in-a-box. "The prisoner is delivered into the hands of our trusty and well-beloved Rosa – doll of the first class – for punishment according to the strict law of tit for tat."

I suddenly found myself walking away with my hand in Rosa's. Under one of the big trees Rosa made me sit down, propping me against the trunk as if I should otherwise have fallen, and a box of tea cups came tumbling up to our feet.

"Take a little tea, my love," said Rosa,

pressing a teacup to my lips.

"What are you doing?" roared the Jack-in-a-box at this moment. "You are not punishing her!"

"I am treating her as she treated me," answered Rosa. "I believe that tit for tat is the rule, and that at present it is my turn."

I thanked her gratefully.

"I think you shall go to bed now, dear," she said. And, taking my hand once more, she led me to a big doll's bed.

"You are very kind," I said, "but I am not tired and it will not bear my weight."

"Well, if you will not go to bed I must put you there," said Rosa, and she snatched me up in her arms and laid me down.

Of course it was just as I expected. I had

hardly touched the two little pillows when the woodwork gave way with a crash, and I fell – fell – fell –

As soon as I could, I sat up and felt myself all over. A little stiff, but, as it seemed, unhurt. Oddly enough, I found that I was back under the old tree in the little wood.

Was it all a dream? The toys had vanished, the lights were out, the evening was chilly, and the hole no larger than it was thirty years ago.

I have returned to the spot many times since, but I have never been able to repeat my visit to the Land of Lost Toys.

The Dolls' Hospital

An extract from *The Story of Live Dolls*
by Josephine Scribner Gates

*Janie is having a magical day. Her dolls have come to life, and now
she is peeping out of her gate to see what is happening outside.*

SHE WAS JUST IN TIME to see, coming
slowly down the street, a white,
covered wagon, marked in red letters,
'Dolls' Ambulance.' It was drawn by six
white kittens, who moved along so carefully

32

that Janie decided they must have some very sick patients aboard.

Janie, curious to see what was within, walked around to the back and peeped in at the little open door.

There she saw a sad sight. The wagon was filled with dolls of all sizes, and in such a condition! Arms and legs were off, hair was missing, and some dolls lay with their poor sightless eyes staring up at her, in such a pathetic manner that Janie could hardly keep back the tears.

Each had a trouble. Some told of how their mammas had lost their arms and legs, and how their hair had been off for weeks. Some were sadly neglected, many being wrapped in small bed-quilts and dirty

33

blankets, as they hadn't an outfit to put on.

The dolls told Janie that the Queen of the Dolls had appeared that morning, had gathered them up from their different homes, and was going to take them to a dolls' hospital.

The Queen invited Janie to go with them. Janie ran in to ask her mamma if she could go, and was soon spinning along after them.

They turned into a country road and down a long lane, at the end of which Janie saw a high wall. The Queen told them that the place was called the Doll Farm.

The gate swung open, and when they had all entered, it closed immediately after them. They got out of the ambulance and

34

the Queen led them up a path towards a building with a sign bearing the name:

The Dolls' Hospital

Janie was too much astonished at the sight that met her eyes to follow. All she could see was an orchard of low trees, whose branches hung full of doll clothes, swaying in the cool morning air. There were tiny undergarments and dresses of all colours. She reached out to examine a particularly pretty one, and to see just how it was made, when a voice startled her.

"Don't touch that. It isn't ripe yet."

"Ripe?" said Janie. "Is it growing?"

"Why, of course. Now see. The button holes aren't begun yet, and these buttons aren't near tight enough. It will be about two weeks before that frock can be picked. Now here is one that I can pick tomorrow," and he explained to Janie just how he could tell when it was ready to be removed from the tree.

Then the gardener, for it was he, showed her the trees full of underwear and little petticoats, the bushes of different coloured socks, with shoes and slippers to match, and last of all, the tree of hats. They

were the sweetest things, of many
different shapes, and from the end of
each branch hung bright ribbons
of all colours.

Janie seated herself under a
tree, from whose branches
dainty parasols of all different
colours were dancing and
nodding in the breeze.

"Oh, Mr Gardener, can I
have one please?" He said she
might and asked her which one
she wanted.

"That beautiful one – wait a
moment. They are all so sweet!"
Janie finally decided on the blue –
a beauty with lace and forget-me-

nots around the top. The pink one had a wreath of wild roses, and it was hard to give that up, but the blue matched her doll's new dress, and so that decided it. Then the gardener told Janie that she had better go into the hospital and see what they were doing there.

Here Janie found the poor crippled dolls being put in fine shape by little doll nurses, wearing soft grey dresses with white aprons. Legs and arms were being replaced, the blind were made to see with blue eyes and brown, bald heads were covered, and such a wealth of hair did those dolls have – some curly, some braided and with a ribbon, and some hanging straight, for the dolls' mammas to braid or curl as they chose.

When their bodies had finally reached perfection, they went into a bathroom for a bath, and Janie went to help the gardener pick clothes.

Together they wandered about, plucking an outfit for each doll. It was great fun to match the dresses to slippers and stockings, and then to complete the costumes with the proper hats. When they carried the dresses in, what a noise arose! Each doll wanted every dress.

The Queen quieted them and gave clothes to each one, which they soon put on. They looked so sweet, clean and pretty that their own mammas would hardly know them.

When they reached home they found the

yard full of little girls weeping for their lost dolls. But as each doll jumped down and ran to its own mamma, what a chattering and babbling filled the air!

"Who mended you?"

"What lovely hair!"

"Where did you get those clothes?" cried the little girls.

The strange tale that Janie told them of all she had seen, and especially of the clothes growing on trees, seemed too wonderful to be believed, and they envied her such delightful experiences.